The Irish Curse

by Martin Casella

A SAMUEL FRENCH ACTING EDITION

SAMUEL FRENCH

FOUNDED 1830

NEW YORK HOLLYWOOD LONDON TORONTO

SAMUELFRENCH.COM

ISBN 78-0-573-69891-0   Printed in U.S.A.   #29694

MUSIC USE NOTE

**IMPORTANT BILLING AND CREDIT
REQUIREMENTS**

THE IRISH CURSE had its world premiere in the New York International Fringe Festival at the Linhart Theater in August 2005, where it won the Overall Excellence Award for Playwrighting. The performance was produced by Craig Zehms and Barry Goralnick and directed by Matt Lenz. The cast was as follows:

FATHER KEVIN SHAUNESSY . . . . .William McCauley

RICK BALDWIN. . . . . .Brian Leahy

JOSEPH FLAHERTY . . . . .Eddie Korbich

STEPHEN FITZGERALD . . . . .Howard Kaye

KEIRAN REILLY . . . . Roderick Hill

THE IRISH CURSE received its Off-Broadway premiere at the SoHo Playhouse in New York City on March 28, 2010. The performance was produced by Craig Zehms and Sarahbeth Grossman, in association with Piglet Productions, Anthony George, and Lawrence Lewis, III; directed by Matt Lenz, costumes by Michael McDonald, lights by Traci Klainer, sound by Walter Trarbach, and scenic design by Lauren Helpern. The cast was as follows:

FATHER KEVIN SHAUNESSY . . . . .Scott Jaeck

RICK BALDWIN. . . . . .Brian Leahy

JOSEPH FLAHERTY . . . . .Dan Butler

STEPHEN FITZGERALD . . . . .Austin Peck

KEIRAN REILLY . . . . Roderick Hill

UNDERSTUDIES . . . . .Patrick James Lynch, Bill Timoney

CHARACTERS

RICK BALDWIN – Early twenties. A smart, optimist, fun-loving Staten Island stud who's studying sports medicine at a local New York college. Rick's the kind of guy who paints his face green, drinks a lot and hangs with his buds on St. Patrick's Day.

JOSEPH FLAHERTY – Forties. On the short side, stout and balding. Born in Savannah, Georgia, he's now an angry, liberal contracts lawyer who lives on the "way Upper West Side." His wife recently walked out, leaving him with two young daughters.

STEPHEN FITZGERALD – Late thirties. Tall, handsome gay cop from the Bronx. He's a moody, dark, taciturn smartass. Lives with his father, who's also a cop. Stephen never ever ever sees the glass as half full, although he would probably like to.

KEVIN SHAUNESSY – Late forties/early fifties. A Catholic priest, originally from Boston. He's the principal of a parochial school in Brooklyn Heights which donates rooms to various support groups. A sweet, caring guy with acting aspirations. Actually looks like he could play a priest on TV.

KEIRAN RILEY – Late twenties. Nice-looking, middle class guy from Queens who works at a roofing company. Keiran is exuberant, very nervous and very sincere. He's also really Irish and someone you'd want to be your best friend.

SETTING

A basement meeting hall. St. Sebastian's Catholic Church in Brooklyn Heights.

TIME

A rainy Wednesday evening. Late September.

AUTHOR'S NOTES

The five guys absolutely should look as if they are of Irish heritage, whether they be redheads, blondes or dark Irish. It is important that Stephen be very good-looking and tall. Joseph needs to be short in stature, balding, and chubby, if possible. Rick should be twenty-two at the very most; he must look as if he runs and plays many sports. Fr. Kevin has to look as if he could play a priest on television: witty, trustworthy, decent, maybe even with steel gray hair. Keiran should be nice-looking, good-humored and sincere.

The play really works when they all look different and are different shapes and sizes.

THE IRISH CURSE is dedicated to the memory of Patrick Quinn, who dedicated his life to improving the lives of actors everywhere.

ACT I

(A small plain meeting hall in Saint Sebastian Catholic Church in Brooklyn Heights. It is about 5:30 on a rainy Wednesday afternoon in late summer. There is a bank of windows on one side of the room and a door on the other.)

(JOSEPH FLAHERTY, an ex-Georgian in his forties, enters the room. He is short, chubby, dressed quite conservatively, and has what under better circumstances would be an Irish choirboy's face. He carries a briefcase. He finds a light switch and turns on the lights. He is followed by **RICK BALDWIN**. **RICK** *is early twenties, well-built, smart, with an expansive, buoyant personality. He searches his backpack as* **JOSEPH** *sets up folding chairs.)*

RICK. So I get on the bus – I'm psyched – I had a pretty cool day – I do the Metrocard thing – I say "how ya doin'" to the driver – he grins, he knows me, he's my bud – and I'm like – where's a seat – cause the frigging bus is packed – stuffed – like full – so I glance all the way to the back seat – and sitting there – like a frigging madonna or something – is –

JOSEPH. OUCH!

(JOSEPH squeals and drops a chair. His furiously grabs his finger. There is rage on his face; he looks as if he has just been thrown into a Dante's seventh circle of Hell.)

RICK. What?!

JOSEPH. I caught my finger – in the goddamn chair – !

RICK. You okay? Is it bleeding?

JOSEPH. Great! I just said "goddamn" in church –

RICK. Let me look at it –

JOSEPH. You're not a doctor!

RICK. Sort of!

JOSEPH. "Sort of!" "Sort of!"

RICK. I know enough to help with a pinched finger.

JOSEPH. *(bending his finger)* It's all right!

RICK. You sure?

JOSEPH. Yes. See!

> *(He wiggles his hand, trying to make it better.)*

> Ouch! Shit! Now I just said shit!

> *(Making a face,* **JOSEPH** *goes back to lining up the chairs. He's making a big show of doing it with a hurt digit.* **RICK** *gets a protein bar and a fruit smoothie from his backpack.)*

RICK. So – coming here – on the bus – I'm looking down the aisle – and there, like a frigging mental vision – there's this babe – this frigging goddess – I mean, hi-ya-momma – Joseph, she is so checking me out – I check her out – she smiles – I smile – I let her know I'm interested – we get off the bus – together – walk through the rain – I chat her up – she's a bonds trader –

JOSEPH. Rick –

RICK. – taking the frigging the bus–

JOSEPH. – are you gonna – ?

RICK. – we go into Starbucks –

JOSEPH. – let me – ?

RICK. – we chat some more –

JOSEPH. – you're not gonna – are you – ?

RICK. Huh?

JOSEPH. – are you going to help me?!?

RICK. *(understanding)* Oh.

JOSEPH. Oh!

RICK. Sorry. I'm an "A" hole.

> *(unwraps the protein bar and helps* **JOSEPH** *with the chairs)*

RICK. Anyway – we have a couple of Frappaccino lattes – they're good – I go into the john – coffee goes right through me – she follows me – she fricking follows me! – We make out in the john – in the john – with release! – Then she gives her number – get this – get this – her name is Wednesday – swear to God – babe's name is Wednesday!

JOSEPH. There's always a babe, isn't there, Rick?

RICK. Huh?

JOSEPH. I mean – you're on the bus, you're on the subway, on your bike, at the gym, at church, Mickey D's –

RICK. I don't do Mickey D's, Joseph. Too greasy. I don't eat fast food –

JOSEPH. There's always a babe. Always checking you out. Always asking you home –

RICK. This sounds like a jealousy issue –

JOSEPH. Don't use that stuff against me!

RICK. You used the stuff about the babes – !

JOSEPH. Because you were talking about babes!

RICK. I was telling you about something that happened.

JOSEPH. Did it, Rick? Did it really happen? Is there really always a babe?

RICK. What's with you?

JOSEPH. I want to know. Is there always a babe? If there is could you steer one in my direction? Introduce me around? Talk me up? Because I swear, if I don't get laid soon, I'm going to fuck that folding chair.

RICK. Joseph – you're in church!

JOSEPH. I already said "shit" and "goddamn."

(**STEPHEN** *enters, soaking wet and in a lousy mood. He loudly announces to the others:*)

STEPHEN. I hate this fucking city.

RICK. Look, Joey, you just need to relax –

JOSEPH. I have told you a million times – do not – on pain of death and disfigurement – do not call me Joey –

RICK. Sorry –

JOSEPH. Italian boys are named Joey. Someone who gets killed by the Mob is named Joey! My name is Joseph. I know it sounds Italian, thereby giving you some tacit permission to shorten it to Joey, but I am Irish and it is Joseph!

RICK. Okay. Joseph. Relax. You'll get laid, bud. It'll happen. Then you'll tell me about it!

JOSEPH. Easy for you to say. You and your "babes."

RICK. Well…I'm a hottie.

JOSEPH. Don't mess up what you got at home. Okay? All that screwing around behind her back. That girl loves you. She doesn't care about your limitations. Or your shortcomings –

RICK. Bite me, choir boy!

JOSEPH. What?!

RICK. My *limitations* – !

JOSEPH. I didn't mean it like that –

RICK. My *short*comings – !

JOSEPH. Ricky, come on, it's just a figure of – !

STEPHEN. You two are like a couple of old queens –

RICK. You don't even know what this is all about – !

STEPHEN. I don't give a shit – both of ya – just shut your fucking traps!!

JOSEPH. And what are you gonna do if we don't? Handcuff us? Take us over to the station house? *Shoot* us? Here. Let me go for my wallet so you got an *excuse*!

STEPHEN. *(He sits, takes out an iPhone and taps away on it.)* Know something, Joseph? When I met you – I thought you were a fag –

JOSEPH. You *what?*

RICK. Oh, God –

STEPHEN. I thought you were a big ol' queer –

RICK. We're *never* gone hear the end of this!

STEPHEN. A *major* homo sissy boy –

JOSEPH. And why did you think that, Stephen?

RICK. 'Cause you're a priss ass –

STEPHEN. Naw, that's not it –

RICK. 'Cause he wouldn't screw his wife so she dumped him for another guy?

JOSEPH. You Yankee piece of shit – !

STEPHEN. *(mockingly)* We're in a *church*, for Chrissake!

RICK. Z'at why?!

STEPHEN. No, Staten Island Ferry Boy, that's not why –

RICK. Then *what*?!!

STEPHEN. Queers don't like their names to be shortened. They want to be called by their entire name. Not Joey or Joe. *Joseph.* Not Mike or Mikey. *Michael.*

JOSEPH. Not Steve or Stevie.

(pointedly)

Stephen.

STEPHEN. Yeah.

JOSEPH. Well I'm *not* gay.

STEPHEN. Duh.

JOSEPH. What's *that* supposed mean?

STEPHEN. It means "duh."

JOSEPH. I know it means "duh." What did you *mean* by "duh."

RICK. He meant "duh."

JOSEPH. But what's "duh" supposed to *mean*?

STEPHEN. It means "duh."

(grinning at him)

Duh.

JOSEPH. You think just 'cause you're so handsome – because you are so goddamn good-looking –

STEPHEN. I'm tall, too – don't forget tall –

JOSEPH. Well, you can't talk to me like that!

STEPHEN. Like what, Joseph? I just said "duh." It meant like, "Obviously you're not gay." You have – *had* – a wife. You got two kids. You have terrible taste in clothes, you're a real estate attorney, you drive a Jetta and you live in Inwood. Duh.

(**JOSEPH** *realizes he has on his suit coat. He removes it and places it over the back of the chair.* **RICK** *sees this, he takes off his own rain poncho.* **JOSEPH** *sits in a chair. Nobody says anything for a moment.*)

JOSEPH. It's 'cause I'm from Savannah.

STEPHEN. What?

JOSEPH. That's why you thought I was gay. Men from Savannah are gentlemen. We speak softly. We use proper English. We're *genteel*. Genteel men are often mistaken for gay.

STEPHEN. Wasn't the first time, huh?

JOSEPH. Oh, you are just hateful.

(**STEPHEN** *taps away on his iPhone.*)

STEPHEN. You know what, Joseph? I can relate. Big butch cops are often mistaken for *straight*.

JOSEPH. Most of them *are*!

STEPHEN. Not *all*.

JOSEPH. That oughta teach you not to judge a book by –

STEPHEN. *(looking at his phone)* All right!!!

RICK. What?

STEPHEN. I just got a date –

RICK. A "date?"

STEPHEN. What do you want me to say, Rick. "I'm gonna blow some guy after group?"

JOSEPH. Did you hear what I said, Steven? I hope you learned a good lesson today I hope you remember it.

STEPHEN. "Yes, dear."

JOSEPH. You quit that. I don't like that gay boy talk.

STEPHEN. That's not what you said last night. When I was on my knees –

JOSEPH. Stop it. Right now! Rick'll think you're serious.

RICK. Yeah, right. Like Stephen would blow *you.*

JOSEPH. What's *that* supposed to mean?!!

RICK. Whattaya think!

STEPHEN. Oh, no – not again! Don't even start!

RICK. *(after a beat; making it up to him)* Joseph – my girlfriend is thinking about law school. You like being a lawyer?

JOSEPH. It's all right. Wouldn't tell my kids to do it –

RICK. You don't seem like any lawyers I know.

JOSEPH. How many lawyers is *that?*

RICK. Well…I know some law students.

JOSEPH. I mostly just do contracts.

RICK. You just don't seem like the lawyers on tv.

JOSEPH. Because they're on *tv.*

STEPHEN. He's a *real* lawyer –

RICK. You don't seem very arrogant.

JOSEPH. Lawyers aren't arrogant!

STEPHEN. Not on Planet Joseph –

RICK. *All* the lawyers on tv are arrogant – or neurotic.

STEPHEN. *(to* **JOSEPH***)* You're two for two.

JOSEPH. *(to* **RICK***)* Those are actors. They're *acting.* It's not like that in a courtroom.

RICK. I met a babe in a courtroom once –

JOSEPH. Of course you did.

RICK. She was a bailiff. She was hot.

STEPHEN. I met a hot bailiff once.

RICK. Yeah?

STEPHEN. Online. Went to his house. He had one of those little machines they write on –

JOSEPH. He wasn't a bailiff. He was a court *stenographer.*

STEPHEN. Maybe the other guy was a bailiff –

RICK. The "other" guy –

STEPHEN. He had a roommate –

JOSEPH. I don't think I wanna hear this –

STEPHEN. After we all finished, I got up. The bailiff started to laugh. He said I musta been lying on the steno machine. I had the keyboard imprinted over my ass. So I made the stenographer type on me.

(A boyish-looking man of about 50 enters. He is in a priest's collar and uniform. This is **FATHER KEVIN SHAUNESSY**. *Behind* **KEVIN**, *in the doorway, is a sexy young Irishman in his late twenties,* **KEIRAN RILEY**.*)*

KEVIN. These are the other guys – Keiran, come on inside.

RICK. Yeah, we don't bite.

STEPHEN. *(eyeing* **KEIRAN**) Unless you *ask* –

KEVIN. Gentlemen, this is Keiran. Stephen. Joseph. And –

RICK. *(extending his hand to* **KEIRAN**) Rick. Rick Baldwin.

KEIRAN. *(with an Irish lilt)* Are you one of *the* Baldwins?

RICK. Naw. But I did meet Alec once. You know, like in person, he has chest hair growing up to his chin?

KEIRAN. Does he?

RICK. Yeah, he's a freak.

KEIRAN. I like his performances in the fillums.

STEPHEN. *(shaking* **KEIRAN**'s *hand)* You really are Irish.

KEIRAN. Reilly on my father's side. Gallagher on me mum's.

STEPHEN. Dad was a Fitzgerald. Ma was a Rice.

KEIRAN. Do you know their counties?

STEPHEN. Naw. We're like fourth generation.

KEIRAN. You're an awfully big lad, Stephen. What do you do? Some sort of sport?

STEPHEN. I'm an undercover cop. We track down illegals. You got a green card?

KEIRAN. Well, I – I – I have it right here – somewhere –

STEPHEN. Kidding, guy! It was a joke!

(pause)

Like I would bust a woof like you.

KEIRAN. A "woof?"

KEVIN. *(knows where this is going)* It's an American expression, Keiran. It means – a –

STEPHEN. *(interrupting, laying on the charm)* A pal. A bud. Like someone you just met.

KEIRAN. Oh. I like that. A woof.

STEPHEN. *(looking at him, like a dog)* Woof!

KEVIN. Stephen –

RICK. Down boy.

KEIRAN. *(shaking hands)* Joseph. Right?

JOSEPH. That's correct.

KEIRAN. Are you – ?

JOSEPH. My daddy's people were Flahertys. My poor mama was a Mulrooney. Oil and water! Oil and water! Mama used to say living with a Flaherty was like living with your own black cloud. She walked right out when I was fourteen. Said it was that or hanging herself and being a good Catholic she just couldn't find it in her heart to commit a mortal sin with no possibility of redemption. I hated her at the time but I have come to see she was acting not out of selfishness but self-preservation. She was an *exceptional* woman.

KEIRAN. *(not expecting that much detail)* I'm sure she was.

KEVIN. Well. I guess that's everybody. We should start. I'll make the speech.

STEPHEN. *(as they all sit)* Do you need to?

KEVIN. It's required when we have someone new.

RICK. Oh you just like making speeches!

   (to **KEIRAN***)*

   Father Kevin does a little acting. On the side.

KEIRAN. Does he now?

STEPHEN. Oh yeah.

KEVIN. Stephen –

STEPHEN. He was on *Law and Order* last week.

RICK. Playing a priest!

JOSEPH. He was *very* good.

KEVIN. It was only a few lines. One scene. We were in the courtroom. I had heard this young hoodlum's confession and they wanted me to break my vows and repeat what he had said but I wouldn't.

(*pause*)

I got to cry.

KEIRAN. I saw it! You were good!

KEVIN. It's the third time I've been on. Haven't had a top of the show credit yet. There's always next season.

KEIRAN. Do you mind me asking – did you make good money?

KEVIN. Yeah. I'm going to use it to get new pictures. Okay. Here's the speech. I think you'll appreciate hearing it.

KEIRAN. Especially from a film star.

KEVIN. Not really a film star –

KEIRAN. Well a telly star, then!

KEVIN. (*taking a moment, preparing, doing his "speech"*) Good evening, everyone. I'm Father Kevin Shaunessy.

RICK, STEPHEN, JOSPEH. Hi, Father Kevin.

KEVIN. I'm the pastor here at Saint Sebastians. And I'd like to welcome you all tonight. This is a *support* group. That's why we're all here. I will be acting as moderator. There's a phone list on the table. My number's there if need it. Add yours if there're any changes. Now. You'll each take a turn. Talk about what's on your mind this week. And oh – please turn off your cellphones. A couple of rules. This is a house of God. No profanity. You can talk about whatever you *need* to but try to exercise a little good taste and discretion –

STEPHEN. That's directed at me.

KEIRAN. Is it?

STEPHEN. I have a sex addiction. I go to *that* group on Tuesdays.

KEIRAN. You have a sex addiction in addition to – ?

STEPHEN. Yeah. Probably *because* of it.

KEVIN. Keiran, I know this is uncomfortable for you but I think you should start. Tell us about how you found us and – uhm – well – just go ahead –

*(**KEIRAN** sits there in silence for a long time. His mouth is dry and he isn't sure what to say.)*

KEVIN. Take your time.

KEIRAN. Do I have to say *everything?*

KEVIN. As much as you feel comfortable sharing.

KEIRAN. I mean, you want to know about my – my –

KEVIN. Well – if you – want to – talk about it –

KEIRAN. Jesus, Mary, and Joseph…

(horrified)

In detail?! Like a description?!

KEVIN. No. NO! Just your feelings *about* it.

KEIRAN. Oh, thank God!

STEPHEN. Damn.

KEVIN. Ste-phen.

STEPHEN. It's what I live for.

*(**KEVIN** takes a moment to get on track.)*

KEVIN. Well then. Okay. Keiran.

(like he's on a set)

"Action!"

*(Silence. **KEIRAN** looks at **JOSEPH**.)*

KEIRAN. How do I start?

JOSEPH. You can sit or stand –

KEIRAN. I'll sit.

RICK. Introduce yourself, say why you're here.

KEIRAN. Don't know if I can –

RICK. What?

KEIRAN. Say the words – out loud –

KEVIN. Keiran, that's the point of the group. When you say things out loud, they lose their power.

KEIRAN. Can someone else go first, please? So I can see how it's done.

KEVIN. Well –

KEIRAN. Just this once!

RICK. All right! Look! *I'll* do it! I'll go!

KEIRAN. Thank you, Rick.

RICK. Hi. My name is Rick. Don't do the "Hi, Rick" thing. I'm twenty-two years old. I live on Staten Island. I go to Staten Island College. I'm studying sports medicine. And the reason I'm here is because I got a small dick. I mean really small. *Really*. Small. Like *small*. Like from the children's menu. Growing up, I always heard it called the Irish Curse. It mostly only happens to us full-blooded Irish guys. Not *all* full-blooded Irish guys because my best bud Dylan is full-blooded Irish and he's hung like giraffe.

(to KEIRAN*)*

We take showers together. After b-ball. Trust me. The Curse runs in my family. My father's got it. So do both my bros. One of them actually tried to off himself 'cause of it. Dumb fuck.

(to KEVIN*)*

Sorry.

(back to KEIRAN*)*

He's okay now. The freak. He took pills. Everything I read about guys with small dicks goes on and on about how it's "all in their head" and "it doesn't make a difference" and my personal favorite, that "it ain't the meat it's the motion" bullshit – sorry, Father – I just get really pissed off because those guys writing those columns are obviously walking around with a Happy Meal in their pants. And I would like to have dragged their collective asses down to the hospital where my bro was lying there with a tube down his throat and make them tell him to his face the size of his dick doesn't matter. It matters! It matters to me. It matters to him.

It matters to all us guys who got royally fucked in that department. And Father, I'm not going to apologize for saying fucked. When I was growing up – I only ever saw my dad and my bros – so I never thought I was different from the other guys. Then when I got to middle school – that's when I found out I was a frigging freak –

KEVIN. Rick. Self esteem.

RICK. Yeah. Right. Self esteem. "I am not my penis." I only *think* I am. I have a lot of trouble not going there – to that dark place. I'm working on it. I even got my dad and both my bros working on it. But they're Irish. Optimism is not exactly a word in their dictionary. I love what I do. Studying the sports medicine. I'm a sports nut. B-ball. Hockey. I run. Hanging around with athletes I learned this trick. I thought they were kidding but they all do it. *Wear a jock.* Always. Under your street clothes. Especially under *jeans.* It takes what you got. Shoves it up front and center. And I stuff it. A sock. Nice white sports tube. Loosely rolled. Great basket, huh?

*(modeling for **KEIRAN**)*

It's an illusion but most of Manhattan's walking around with more than what God gave 'em. Anyway. That's my sad story. Boo-hoo. "A million guys out there like me." "Least I got a penis." "It works, doesn't it?" "Yes it does." Any other comments and questions can be e-mailed to me at "Rick-I-Got-A-Small-Dick".com. *Real* website.

(making a fist, raising it)

Self-esteem!

KEVIN. Thank you, Rick.

RICK. Sure. Happy to do it, Father.

KEVIN. You can sit down now.

KEIRAN. Wait.

RICK. Huh?

KEIRAN. You never said *why* you were here?

STEPHEN. Because his schlong is the size of baby corn.

KEIRAN. Really and truly?

RICK. Wanna see it?

KEIRAN. I'll take your word.

RICK. Anything else?

KEIRAN. How'd you find this place?

RICK. There was an article in the Village Voice. Last spring. About self-help support groups. At the end of the article it mentioned Fr. Kevin. In this jokey sorta way – like "Places We Wouldn't Be Caught Dead But For You Poor Freaks Who Need It."

(pause)

Because of what happened to my brother, I cut the article out and kept it in a drawer next to my bed. I was gonna show it to him, but – I kept it for me. Saved it for a month. Until I could work up the nerve to come by here. Stood across the street for three Wednesday nights. Then I finally – walked in.

KEIRAN. Good for you.

RICK. Can I sit down now?

KEIRAN. I was just wondering – do you have trouble with girls – and they way they respond to you?

JOSEPH. Are you kidding? This one's got "babes" hanging all over him. You should hear the stories he tells.

KEIRAN. The ladies – they don't mind – when they find out – it's a sports sock?

RICK. None of them so far.

KEIRAN. And there's been a great number of them. From what –

JOSEPH. Joseph.

KEIRAN. *Joseph* here says.

RICK. Yeah.

KEIRAN. And your size was never a problem?

RICK. No.

KEIRAN. I'm glad to hear it.

RICK. Now can I –

KEIRAN. Is there one special girl?

RICK. Yep.

KEIRAN. What does she think?

RICK. She's cool.

KEIRAN. And sexually – ?

RICK. We make it work.

KEIRAN. Have you been together long?

RICK. Four years.

KEIRAN. Again. Good for you.

> *(pause)*

> Does she know about the other women?

> *(off **RICK**'s head shake)*

> I see.

RICK. Finished?

KEIRAN. One last question.

STEPHEN. You from a frigging newspaper?

KEIRAN. I just want to know –

KEVIN. Keiran, maybe we should –

RICK. Let him ask. I mean it's fine. It's why we're here, right?

KEVIN. Go ahead.

KEIRAN. What do you plan to do about it? Your problem?

RICK. We don't call it a problem –

JOSEPH. It's one of Father Kevin's rules –

STEPHEN. It's our "situation."

KEVIN. "Because if you call it a problem – "

STEPHEN, RICK, JOSEPH, KEVIN. " – IT *IS* ONE!"

KEIRAN. All right. Your situation, then.

RICK. What do you mean? What can I do?

KEIRAN. Have you tried one of those vacuum pump thingies?

STEPHEN. Oh Jesus –

KEVIN. Stephen –

STEPHEN. This really is your first time, huh, kid?

KEIRAN. I've seen the advertisements – in the magazines –

STEPHEN. Those vacuum things are for shit. Trust me.

KEIRAN. And the stretching exercises – with the weights?

JOSEPH. Lord I tried those once. Couldn't walk for a week.

STEPHEN. Yeah and it obviously gave him a gigantic cock – otherwise he wouldn't be here –

KEIRAN. And the fat injections?

RICK. They make your dick all lumpy and lopsided. I'll keep my teeny weeny perfect prick.

KEIRAN. What about the operation? Where they –

STEPHEN. Cut the ligaments at the base of your cock so that the other eight inches that're supposedly shoved up inside just drops down, miraculously turning you into Johnny "Wadd" Holmes? – I don't think so.

KEIRAN. Why not?

STEPHEN. Because if something goes wrong, you can't get hard. *Ever again.* Or your cock gets twisted all around. Or you get an infection. Or you bleed to death –

KEIRAN. So what you're saying is there's nothing?

STEPHEN. Not unless you want to spend a king's ransom *and* take a chance on permanently disfiguring yourself.

RICK. Or worse. I'm sitting.

KEVIN. There's this, Keiran. That's why we're here.

KEIRAN. But –

STEPHEN. You did your homework, kid. The questions you studied for just weren't on the test.

(*pause*)

All that shit about the truth will set you free. The truth is just one more kick in the ass.

(**KEIRAN** *is silent. The guys give him a moment, then* –)

KEVIN. Who's next?

(**STEPHEN**, *staring at* **KEIRAN**, *suddenly stands up.*)

STEPHEN. My name is Stephen –

JOSEPH & RICK. *(like an AA meeting)* Hi, Stephen!

STEPHEN. I'm thirty-eight years old, I'm a NYPD cop and I got a dick the size of a cocktail wiener. You know the ones that come in those little cans? I actually bought one of those cans once and tried to fit my dick inside. And I could! I'm fag, too, and a fag with a puny prick is like a bull with tits. "Whattaya do with it?" Heard that in the station house locker room. Said by a brother cop. *And a brother fag.* Who's Polish. You all know what they say about Polacks.

KEVIN. Stephen –

STEPHEN. I'm not ethnic stereotyping or racial profiling or whatever – but when something's true it's true – and I've slept with my share of Polacks – most Polacks got big cocks and most Micks don't. *That*'s why they call it the Irish Curse –

KEVIN. Okay – you are way outta line –

STEPHEN. Yeah, well – that's what makes me Stephen.

JOSEPH. Get over yourself!

KEVIN. We're supposed to help Keiran feel better, not worse.

STEPHEN. Right. Right. I forgot. *That*'s why we're here!

(It takes a moment – **STEPHEN** *defiantly backs down.)*

KEVIN. What was your week like?

STEPHEN. I busted a bunch a Korean guys selling batteries on the A train. That was important. I sent a family of nine, including twin two-year-olds, back to Guatemala where they'll get killed by death squads. Then my partner and I –

(to **KEIRAN***)*

Cop partner, not – you know – well, you don't – I don't have a partner-partner. I live at home. With my father. Who's a cop. That's *another* story. We did surveillance on this East Side couple who have an illegal maid from Thailand whose passport they've taken away and are making live in a closet –

JOSEPH. Oh Stephen, that's just awful –

RICK. You bust 'em?

STEPHEN. Yeah but they'll get off. Maid'll get deported. Guy's an asshole, a hedge fund manager who's worth about eighty gazillion dollars *and* pals with the Mayor – and he's paying this girl – because she *is* a girl – she is seventeen – only a few years younger than our friend Ricky here – oh, a dollar-fifty an hour for a 24/7 job – *when* they pay her – did I mention that the wife gets off by slapping our Thai friend around?

KEIRAN. Really and truly?

STEPHEN. You say that a lot.

KEIRAN. My mother says it a lot.

STEPHEN. You a mama's boy?

KEIRAN. I respect and honor my mother.

STEPHEN. But are you a mama's boy?

KEIRAN. If you're asking me am I gay. No. I'm not.

STEPHEN. Just wanted to know.

KEVIN. *Something* good must have happened to you this week.

STEPHEN. Yeah but I got more crappy stuff. My father asked me again when am I going to bring home a nice girl? I just keep saying, "Dad, you know what a cop's life is like. When would I have time to meet a nice girl?" Unless she's *Thai.*

(*suppresses a wave of anger, then continues*)

Dad says that all the other cops he knows – and he knows – oh – thousands of cops – are all married and happy and have kids – and he just wants me to be married and happy and have kids. I hug him and say "Thank you, Dad, I love you, you're my best friend." Then I kiss him goodnight and go upstairs and jerk off to naked pictures of Derek Jeter –

RICK. You have *naked* pictures of Jeter?

STEPHEN. The Internet is an *amazing* thing.

RICK. How do you find this shit?

(He glances over at **KEVIN.***)*

Sorry –

STEPHEN. It's all out there. Jeter, A-Rod, Wes Welker –

RICK. Welker?

STEPHEN. Yeah.

RICK. Posed dick shots of Welker?!

STEPHEN. He didn't *pose.* Some whackjob'll sneak a cell-phone camera into the locker room – bam – an hour later – there's Welker's tight end –

JOSEPH. THIS IS NOT WHY WE ARE HERE!

RICK. Yeah, yeah, Joseph, okay, okay – I mean – it's just I know there's porn for guys – straight guys – but gay porn – of *sports* stars – ?!

STEPHEN. Well, it's not like there's a *lot* of it – but what's there is fucking –

KEVIN. Stephen –

STEPHEN. Yeah, okay. So after I lope the mule, I clean up, climb into bed and I lie there, thinking about my life. I'm in good shape. I'm handsome. I'm smart. Most people don't think cops are smart. They *are.* I even have a Master's degree. I never told you guys that before. Police science. But the thing that really makes me nuts – the thing I got going through my head is – *why the fuck did God make me so tall?*

(to **KEIRAN***)*

Because the absolute worst thing about being – "an awfully big lad" – is guys expect you to be "awfully big" everywhere. You should see their faces when they finally get a look. I mean, they're expecting Captain Huge, right? That guy must have the Gay Holy Grail in his shorts. Paul Bunyon *and* Babe the Blue Ox. What they get is a *bull with tits.*

KEVIN. *(after an appropriate silence)* So what was the good part of your week?

STEPHEN. I had fantastic sex with four guys. One in the back room of a bar on West Street. Two woofs from Italy that I met in a gay bookstore. And a Catholic priest in Soho who was hearing my confession.

KEIRAN. You had sex with a priest?

STEPHEN. I blew him. Neat, clean – five minutes, it's over.

KEIRAN. You don't let them do anything back?

STEPHEN. Would *you?*

KEIRAN. Do you ever give them a chance?

STEPHEN. To what? Discover that the humpy stud is packing a popgun and not a pistol? That's what sex is for me, okay? They get off – I go home. No names, no numbers –

KEIRAN. No future.

STEPHEN. That's why I go to the other group, Keiran. Okay? We don't talk about *that* part of it here.

KEIRAN. How'd you find the group? *This* one.

STEPHEN. Stroke shots of Jeter aren't the only thing on line. One day I was feeling particularly sorry for myself so I typed in "The Irish Curse." That led me to Saint Sebastian's and Kevin's homepage.

KEIRAN. You don't seem like the type who'd go to a meeting.

STEPHEN. No. I don't.

KEIRAN. Then why –

KEVIN. Keiran –

STEPHEN. Naw, it's okay. I'll tell him.

    (to **KEIRAN***)*

I came for sex. It's always about sex.

KEVIN. Well thank you, Stephen, for that very illuminating –

KEIRAN. Wait –

STEPHEN. Here he goes again –

RICK. Watch it, Stephen, he's got his pad –

KEIRAN. I just want to know one thing.

JOSEPH. That's what you said before.

KEIRAN. It's a discussion, is it not?

KEVIN. Yes.

KEIRAN. Then why aren't we allowed to *discuss?*

KEVIN. The point is for people to talk about themselves, unburden their feelings, get it all out –

KEIRAN. You sound like the fella on the telly –

KEVIN. *(pleased)* Which one?

KEIRAN. The program where the lads come on and say they've shagged their mums. No offense, Father, but I think what you've just said is a load of crap – this fella here just said he's had sexual relations with a priest and none of you batted an eye. He's had sex with all sorts of strangers whose names he doesn't even know – and no one said a word!

KEVIN. Keiran, we're not here to judge –

KEIRAN. I've said nothing about judging. It's not my place. But you'd think one of you would *challenge* him. Not over being gay, I couldn't give a shyte if he were a gay. But over the fact he's clearly lonely and hurting inside and no one seems to care!

JOSEPH. We've just heard all this before –

KEIRAN. Jesus – if this is what he tells *you* – what does he say to the sex addiction fellas?!!

KEVIN. Look, Keiran, we're just here to listen, okay? It's about listening.

KEIRAN. Really and truly?

STEPHEN. *(mocking him)* "Really and truly."

KEIRAN. *(standing to go)* As I said. It's all a load of shyte. You're all just shyte shovelers.

KEVIN. Keiran –

KEIRAN. I didn't come to sit and listen to a bunch of silly buggers complain about their lives. I thought this was a place I might get some advice. Some help! Not *silence!*

(That's all he gets.)

Well. There. As I've just said.

(He starts to go. **STEPHEN** *stops him.)*

STEPHEN. Sit the fuck down.

KEIRAN. I beg your pardon –

STEPHEN. I said – sit the fuck down.

KEVIN. Stephen, I'm not going to tell you again –

STEPHEN. Oh, Jesus, Father. God doesn't care. It's just a stupid fucking word.

(to **KEIRAN***, staring him down)*

What bothered you so much? About what I said.

KEIRAN. The part about not knowing their names. I can't imagine giving myself to a woman, exposing myself that way, making that sort of *connection* – without at least knowing who she is. What she's like. Where she's from. I couldn't do it. I wasn't judging you, Stephen. It's just something I don't understand. How long does it take to ask someone their name?

(Moments pass.)

STEPHEN. I dated a guy once – it was like our third date – we hadn't done anything but kiss – believe it or not – so we go to his place – we start making out – I'm running my hand over his crotch, you know, like – he started getting all excited – he slipped off his pants – then his bikini briefs – I stopped what I was doing and just stared. The guy was frigging huge – huge – I mean – not like scary huge or anything – good huge – it wasn't just big, it was so beautiful –

(stops, remembering it all)

This guy was so sweet – not like most guys you meet with big cocks – jerks who think they own the world 'cause God decided to Supersize their dick – this guy was funny – and gentle and cute and smart – I should have told him all those things and I really wanted to – but all I could say was how hot his cock was – how it was so sexy – and how lucky he was to have it. He gave me this look – he shrugged – and said, "It's genetics,

Stephen. That's all. Genetics." So I asked him if his father had a killer cock, too, and he said no, it was just average, but what did that matter – it just meant that someone, somewhere in his gene pool had the right DNA code and so he got this big cock – it was like having blue eyes, he said, or a lot of hair in your ears – or being tall. Which he wasn't. I was so intimidated I couldn't take off my pants. He asked why and I said, I'm a big guy, see, and – some big guys got little cocks. I told him about "The Irish Curse" and being a full-blooded Mick.

(to **KEIRAN***)*

It's just a bush, basically. Down there. Shitload of hair and then this stubby little head poking out. Like a fucking troll doll.

KEIRAN. What happened to your date?

STEPHEN. I blew him. He came for like a minute and half. *Buckets.* Guess that's genetic, too.

(pause)

Then I went home. That was the last time I had sex with someone whose name I knew.

KEIRAN. Think he cared?

STEPHEN. That I'm not packing?

KEIRAN. That you were simply different from him?

STEPHEN. It was ages ago, kid –

KEIRAN. You didn't answer my question.

STEPHEN. I don't know. Maybe not. In a perfect world.

(Silence. **KEIRAN** *stares at* **STEPHEN***, then takes off his coat and sits back down.)*

JOSEPH. Stephen, you talk about your penis like it's a gun.

STEPHEN. Give me a fucking break!

JOSEPH. Well, you do!

KEVIN. I noticed that myself, Stephen.

RICK. *(quoting* **STEPHEN***)* "A popgun and not a pistol."

KEVIN. You weren't "packing."

STEPHEN. Well, I am a cop.

KEVIN. Cops carry big guns –

STEPHEN. Give it a rest, Kevin.

KEVIN. I've just wondered why a smart funny gay guy like you wanted to become a cop.

STEPHEN. Don't start picking on cops –

KEVIN. I'm not picking on cops. I'm picking on a *gay* cop.

STEPHEN. There are lots of gay cops.

KEVIN. That wasn't my point.

STEPHEN. You think I'm a cop because I get to carry a *big* gun?

RICK. You know what they say about guys who drive big cars?

(He holds his pinkie out to STEPHEN *in the universal sign for "little penis.")*

KEVIN. When you think about it, Stephen, there's a hell of a lot of Irish cops in New York City.

STEPHEN. This is insulting to me and my brother officers.

KEVIN. Just something to think about. Next?

STEPHEN. You can't just do that.

KEVIN. What?

STEPHEN. *That*! Imply I became a police officer to make up for the fact I have a small dick!

KEVIN. I never said that.

STEPHEN. I'm insulted. And that remark about the rest of the Irish cops in New York? Well, you just insulted all of them, *too*. And, Kevin, your argument doesn't hold water because there are a lot of *Italian* cops. And we all know about *Italians*!!!

KEVIN. No, Stephen, what we do *all* know about Italians?

STEPHEN. Well, in my experience –

RICK. Here come the ethnic stereotypes!

STEPHEN. It's not a stereotype, Rick, it's *true*! Wops are *all* well-hung!

RICK. *(mock serious)* But the Chinese *aren't.*

JOSEPH. But Polacks, Estonians and Latvians *are!*

KEVIN. *(He's right with them.)* But Spaniards *aren't.*

RICK. But Israelis *are!*

JOSEPH. And Saudis *aren't.*

KEVIN. But Austrians *are!*

RICK. And Greeks *aren't.*

JOSEPH. But Swedes *are!*

KEVIN. But Japanese *aren't!*

STEPHEN. WELL, THEY'RE NOT!!!!

> *(The guys laugh. The game makes them all giddy. Except* **STEPHEN***, who looks like they're crazy.)*

RICK. French-Canadians *are!*

JOSEPH. Koreans *aren't!*

KEVIN. Mexicans *are!*

RICK. The Swiss *aren't!*

JOSEPH. Russians *are.*

KEIRAN. Guys from England certainly *aren't!*

KEVIN. Germans –

JOSEPH, RICK. *Are!*

RICK. Australians?

JOSEPH, KEVIN. *Aren't!*

KEVIN. The Dutch?

EVERYONE BUT STEPHEN. *Are!*

RICK. Albanians?

EVERYONE BUT STEPHEN. *Aren't!*

JOSEPH. *(They are all nearly hysterical by now.)* North Africans?

EVERYONE BUT STEPHEN. *Are!*

KEIRAN. South Africans?

EVERYONE BUT STEPHEN. *Aren't!*

RICK. Black men?

EVERYONE BUT STEPHEN. *Are!*

JOSEPH. White men?

EVERYONE BUT STEPHEN. *Aren't!*

KEVIN. Eskimos?

KEIRAN. Give 'em a break, lads – it's cold up there!

RICK. I think we left out the Pygmies – !

STEPHEN. *(doesn't think this is funny)* Never fucked one –

JOSEPH. Maybe you should –

KEIRAN. I've heard they're *huge*!

JOSEPH. *(raucously teasing* **STEPHEN***)* And not "scary huge" – "beautiful" huge! Beautiful!!!

(**STEPHEN** *realizes how ridiculous he's sounded but won't admit it. The others laugh until they're spent.*)

KEVIN. Now that we have *that* out of our system –

KEIRAN. God that was grand –

JOSEPH. My side hurts – I think I have a stitch –

KEVIN. You all right, Joseph?

JOSEPH. I don't know –

KEVIN. Walk it off. Walk it off.

STEPHEN. *(against his will; knowing he's lost the argument)* First – fuck you all. Okay, so maybe what I said about Italians was dumb –

RICK. Especially since half the guys on my b-ball team are Italian and I've seen them totally naked and you are so full of it. Half of them are teeny!!

STEPHEN. Seriously?

RICK. Trust me, Stephen – in that locker room, we got a *field* of baby corn.

STEPHEN. Yeah?

RICK. Yeah. And we got a Chinese guy with a beer can dick and a black guy who's always saying his wife needs a microscope to find it –

STEPHEN. Okay – I know- it's just easier to think that way – to say that –

RICK. Micks got cursed and Wops got blessed and guys from Lithuania need a handcart to lug it around.

KEIRAN. It's just a way of not making them people, Stephen. They're just objects. They're just their willies.

STEPHEN. Most guys *are* just their willies –

KEIRAN. I don't believe that.

RICK. Neither do I. But I *do* think guys and their dicks have gotten us into a lot of trouble –

JOSEPH. How so?

RICK. I think a lot of guys are really screwed up – about the size of their dicks – I mean, it's mostly guys who run the world, right? – and you know that every single one of them wishes he was bigger – even guys who are *huge* always want another inch or two –

JOSEPH. And when you add in a little testosterone, no wonder we have guns and wars and bombs and terrorists – I mean, just look at the Middle East! You wanna sit those folks down and slap them all silly! How long have those Arabs and Jews been killing each other? And what for? Religion??! Land??!!

KEIRAN. It's the same in the Northern Ireland! With the Catholics and the bloody Protestants!

JOSEPH. Let's be honest, folks. It's not religion they've been fighting over. It's not land! What it boils down to is they're terrified that the Catholic next door or the Arab down the road's got a bigger *weenie*!

KEIRAN. Which is daft because most of the guys in Ireland think they got "The Curse" –

KEVIN. Guys, guys, let's get back on track –

JOSEPH. I think, underneath, war's always been about *that* – don't you? I mean, medieval Europe against Islam, Commies against the West. I mean, why do you think people are still so upset about Vietnam? Really now, what does losing to a bunch of little Asian men in pajamas say about the size and power of the all-American wiener?

RICK. Joseph, you're brilliant!

JOSEPH. Ricky, it's *all* just a pissing contest – !

KEIRAN. And what's a pissing contest but a chance to drop trou and show the other fella what you've got!

JOSEPH. And there's *always* someone bigger and THAT's the fella you hate. You *despise* him. You want him to die in a fiery car crash going ninety miles an hour on the expressway. You want to drop missiles on his mosque! Blow up his buildings! Kill his women! Not because you hate him – oh no! Because you hate the size of his *dick*. Because it's *longer* and *thicker* and *harder* and *hairier* –

STEPHEN. Go, Joseph!!

JOSEPH. What do you think the South is all about! What do you think those pick-up trucks are about? And Confederate flags and swords and guns. They can't even admit they lost a war that was over *over* a hundred and forty years ago because it would mean some G.D. Yankee had a bigger wiener!

RICK. *(delighted with this; grinning)* Have some more coffee, Joseph!

JOSEPH. Really, *that's* what war is all about! Mine's bigger! Mine's fatter. Mine shoots farther. Wish they'd start putting *that* in the history books!!!

STEPHEN. They could have an entire chapter just devoted to the "Penises of Presidents Who Got Us Into Wars!" Right?! I mean, who *wouldn't* want to know how big JFK's cock was?

RICK. Can you imagine? Kids would have to get a note from their parents to go to class!!

JOSEPH. I can see George W. Bush sitting in the Oval office going through secret Iraqi files and photographs, having a triple snit fit because ol' Saddam's pecker is twice the size of his!!

STEPHEN. "Holy cow, Condi, Hussein's *hung*!"

JOSEPH. That's why all those idiot Republicans hated President Clinton so much. Because unlike Mr. Bush – what an appropriate name – he didn't have to start *two* wars to show everyone just how *huge* his penis is; he used his Democratic weenie for the reason it was invented!

KEVIN. Okay, Joseph , okay, calm down –

JOSEPH. And now with Obama – all those guys – Mitch McConnell and John Boehner – know how you actually pronounce his name? "Boner!' You know the guy I mean! The one with the spray-on orange tan – he looks like a fucking Oompa-Loompa!

(The guys look at each other – who knew **JOSEPH** *had it in him?)*

JOSEPH. All those arrogant middle-aged white men with bad hair and chicken dicks – they can't stand Obama because he's black. You know what they say about black men, Stephen. He must have a dick the size of Connecticut! That's why they're trying to destroy him. Starting those rumors he's an Arab. That he wasn't born here! That he's a socialist. That he's Hitler. Because they're all so G.D. jealous of Obama and his big dick! Because American men can't stand it when the other guy has what they don't!

KEIRAN. American men – they're bloody competitive – always got to outdo their neighbor – their yards, their homes, those SUVs – !

STEPHEN. God forbid "his" is bigger than "yours!"

KEIRAN. Especially his willie!

JOSEPH. Keiran, you've just defined the American dream!

KEIRAN. Life, liberty and the pursuit of happiness?

JOSEPH. No! A big car, a bigger house and the biggest wiener!

(He stands, facing the others.)

Hi, my name is Joseph Flaherty and I'm forty-three. I'm a contracts lawyer at a big firm in Midtown. I've worked there since I graduated from Columbia twenty years ago. I met my wife at school and she loved the city and that's why we live in New York.

*(***RICK*** *subtly clears his throat.)*

JOSEPH. What's *that* supposed to mean?

RICK. He deserves the whole story –

JOSEPH. I was gonna tell him!

RICK. Like you told the guy last month –

JOSEPH. I didn't trust him!

RICK. Why not?

JOSEPH. He had snaky eyes –

RICK. Joseph, he was *blind*!

JOSEPH. So he *said*!!!

RICK. *He tripped over the frigging chairs*!

JOSEPH. I trip over the frigging chairs! *I'm* not blind!

STEPHEN. Oh for God's sake, you two – !!!

JOSEPH. A year and a half ago, my wife left me. I came home and there was a note saying she was gone and that our little girls were at the babysitters and I should pick them up and feed them the frozen pizza in the fridge. She also said she was leaving me for her Gyrotonics teacher – whom Stephen was thrilled to learn is Italian –

RICK. And has the dick of death –

STEPHEN. Cliché are clichés for a *reason* –

JOSEPH. She went on in the letter to actually describe this fellow's lovemaking abilities. In detail. Then she drew a picture of his penis. It was very realistic. I think she traced it. Then she left a place where I guess I was supposed to draw mine. And underneath she wrote the words – "This should explain everything."

KEIRAN. Jesus, Mary, and Joseph –

RICK. Yeah.

KEIRAN. How could she be so cruel?

STEPHEN. Because Joseph wouldn't have sex with her.

JOSEPH. Why is is it *always* about sex with you?

STEPHEN. Come on, Joseph, you wouldn't fuck your wife!

JOSEPH. Like I said before, you are hateful.

KEIRAN. That's no reason for her to have been so horrid.

JOSEPH. Maybe not.

KEIRAN. Is that when you found your way to the group?

JOSEPH. There was no group yet. You see – Father Kevin's niece babysits for my girls –

KEIRAN. Is that how you two met?

JOSEPH. Yes, sir. After my wife left, Kevin's niece invited me to a Christmas Mass here. Kevin and I hit it off. In two minutes, I was in his office, crying like a baby.

KEVIN. He was so brave – about his girls – his wife – why she left – the drawing –

JOSEPH. I carried it around – showing it to strangers –

KEVIN. You were a mess.

JOSEPH. Well, thank you!

KEVIN. I simply told him he wasn't the only one in the world suffering from The Curse –

JOSEPH. That's when we started the group —

KEIRAN. You started it together?

JOSEPH. On a dare.

KEIRAN. So who dared who?

JOSEPH. I said we should start a group.

KEVIN. I said we never would.

JOSEPH. I said he didn't have the guts to hold it here at the church. We surprised each other.

KEVIN. We've been having meetings since the beginning of the year.

(gently; getting him back on track)

Go on, Joseph. Finish your story.

JOSEPH. I'm in the same situation these guys are. I've learned to be honest about it. My penis, when it's soft, looks like a bottle cap – and erect – it's a little smaller than my thumb. I guess in some parallel universe, that makes me a grower – not a shower.

KEIRAN. A what?

JOSEPH. A grower not a shower.

KEIRAN. Sorry.

RICK. It means your dick is small when it's soft –

JOSEPH. And when it gets hard, it's a *lot* bigger.

KEVIN. Some men would say the reason they're small is because they're growers and not showers.

STEPHEN. Mostly it means they're just small –

RICK. Not all the time –

STEPHEN. Look, Rick, if some guy tells me he's a grower, not a shower – the only thing going up is a red flag –

RICK. Well, in *my* experience –

STEPHEN. Which *friend* are you gonna tell us about this time?

RICK. My running buddy – Andrew McGillan – Irish on both sides – I've seen him in the showers at the gym and he's kinda small and one day I worked up the nerve to tell him about our group – and he was very polite and said, "Thanks, that's very nice, but I'm a grower not a shower." I said, "Okay, great, but if you ever change your mind." So he smiles and says I obviously don't believe him and since we were all alone in the locker room and we're buds, he – uh – well, there's no "Curse" in his family.

STEPHEN. He actually got hard for you?

RICK. Yeah.

STEPHEN. Whoa! Ricky!

RICK. Stephen, there was nothing sexual about it. The guy was defending his honor. Anyway, the point is, you are wrong. Admit it. Okay? Come on. Admit it! I know you consider yourself the ultimate expert on everything that has to do with dicks and size and based on the fact that you've gone down on half the guys in New York City – the ones with *big dicks*, anyway –

STEPHEN. What the hell is that all about – ?

RICK. Look, I was just offended by the fact that you, as a man with a small dick, won't have sex with other guys who have small dicks –

STEPHEN. I didn't say that –

RICK. Yes, you did, Stephen –

STEPHEN. Well, I didn't mean it like that –

RICK. How did you mean it?

STEPHEN. Just that – I really wasn't interested in them if – if they weren't – fuck.

RICK. I think that blows your explanation about why you came here – because you were "looking for sex" – right out the window – because you certainly weren't going to find any guys with big dicks here. You came for the same reason the rest of us did. You're sick and tired of your whole life being about the size of your dick – and you wanted to talk to someone about it – someone who understood just how you felt – but you could never admit *that* – because *that's* what "makes you Stephen."

STEPHEN. *(to* **FATHER KEVIN***)* Who died and left him in charge?

RICK. It's just that he sits there and he's so frigging cynical and above us all and – I try really hard to deal with what I got –

STEPHEN. By fucking every babe who looks at you twice while your girlfriend quietly sits at home?

KEVIN. *(overlapping the following, getting between them)* Gentlemen, that's enough! Back off. That's enough!!!

STEPHEN. I may be a sad lonely blow-job-giving fuck but I'm not cheating on someone I *profess* to love –

RICK. I *do* love her!!

STEPHEN. Then Jesus Christ – how can you do that to her? IT'S DISGUSTING!! YOU MAKE ME FUCKING SICK!!!

*(***RICK*** walks away from the group. Silence. Then –)*

RICK. Okay. Look. You wanna know the truth – for real? All those babes I talk about? I didn't screw a single one of them.

STEPHEN. Like we didn't know that!

JOSEPH. I didn't!

KEVIN. Neither did I!

STEPHEN. Guess you fooled *some* of us!

RICK. I wasn't trying to fool you! I was trying to give you some hope. That's all! 'Cause the babes really do check me out –

STEPHEN. 'Cause you got a fucking sock in your pants!!!!

RICK. At least I'm trying, okay!!!! At least I'm making an effort –

STEPHEN. At *what*!

RICK. At being *happy*! Something you are *completely* incapable of!!

STEPHEN. Like you even know who I am!

RICK. I know who you are. We all do. Keiran spent twenty minutes with you and had you pegged. You are sad. Sad and unhappy and lonely. Lonely like Joseph here is lonely and maybe like Father Kevin's lonely and probably Keiran is lonely, too. Lonely like I was before I met my girl. The stupid thing is that we do it to ourselves. Because we think we're not good enough or worthy enough to be in a relationship because we don't have what all the other guys have. I mean, come on – who wants to have sex with a guy with a baby dick? You obviously don't. How many gay men do you speak for? How many *women*? That's gotta be the tape going through our heads every waking second of the day. Because we're guys and what makes us guys is that we have dicks and balls. And when you think you don't have a dick and balls, you must not be a guy.

STEPHEN. Shoving a sock down your pants makes it all better?

RICK. Not *all* better. But better. Wanna know something else? Those babes who look at me? I love those looks. It makes me feel great. Who gives a rat's ass if it's me they're eyeing or the sports sock?

STEPHEN. But it's a lie!

RICK. Who cares if it's a lie? I'm not *selling* them anything. Just a nice look at a big basket. I've only ever had sex with one woman in my life. Angela. And I would never do anything to hurt her. I look at other women but I always go home to her. She knows that.

STEPHEN. Are you afraid to have sex with other woman?

RICK. I don't have sex with other women because I love my girlfriend. I know that's inconceivable to you but it's true. I'm a nice Irish Catholic boy, Stephen. Little white lies and all.

KEVIN. You two finished?

STEPHEN. *(after a long beat)* I was wrong. Some guys *are* growers, not showers.

(The others relax; looking over at RICK.)

You oughta write gay porn. The story about your buddy at the gym. How big *was* he?

RICK. Soft – two inches. Hard – seven and a half!

STEPHEN. Jee-sus!

(Silence as they all reflect on that.)

KEVIN. And with *that* in mind – Joseph?

JOSEPH. Where was I? Oh yeah…Keiran, I'm shy. I've always been shy. When you're five five and balding at sixteen and got a penis that looks like something you'd pop off a bottle of grape Nehi, you got two choices. You can be one of those Napolean complex nut jobs – or you go the other way – which is to clam up and pretend you don't exist because then no one would ever say anything to you about being short and bald and you stay away from girls because, well, girls are known to like men who can satisfy them and how could a guy with a thumb penis satisfy anyone? So you pray no one will talk to you or ask you any questions and you throw yourself into your work and that's what life is and probably will always be. About work. About being invisible.

KEIRAN. But you were married –

JOSEPH. My crazy wife just took one look at me and fell in love. Don't ask me to explain. She said she liked short guys and that I wasn't a braggart or obnoxious or mean. She liked that I was smart and I could help her with her studies. Which I did. I was so amazed someone could love me like that – I treated her like she was – I don't know – a miracle from God. Which she was –

(remembering)

JOSEPH. *(cont.)* The most amazing thing, Keiran, the absolute most amazing thing was that she loved sex. Not just liked. Loved. Morning, noon, and night. And she didn't care about my size. She was a virgin on our wedding night and didn't know any different –

RICK. She musta thought *all* guys had bottle tops –

STEPHEN. That's ridiculous! She musta seen a statue of David once. A picture in a magazine!

JOSEPH. She wasn't very worldly, Stephen. She'd never seen any porn. She'd never seen an erect penis! I mean, where would she have? Then the world started to change and there were all these naked guys on cable tv and the Internet – I started getting paranoid about what kind of lover I was – we started having less sex – I was never very good at it anyway – my paranoia didn't help – I was just so small I kept slipping out –

STEPHEN. That's the reason I'm alive today!

JOSEPH. How's that?

STEPHEN. I was lousy at sex. I didn't like to receive, you know, and I couldn't give – I mean, you want to fuck the guy, right, not make him laugh – that's when I started getting all paranoid about my size – when I made the decision – I just started doing blow jobs – never having real sex, you know – I think it saved my life, because of AIDS and stuff –

RICK. So the cocktail wiener saved your life, huh?

*(***STEPHEN*** *nods.)*

KEIRAN. Fate's a funny thing.

STEPHEN. I have this friend. He's always bragging about his nine inches of pink steel. What I wouldn't give to just once know what that was like. I mean, there are guys with twelve inches – twelve inches – that's a fucking ruler!

RICK. I can't even imagine –

STEPHEN. I can! Having that between your legs? I mean seriously, take a ruler sometime and hold it at the base of your cock and see where it hits. I mean, it goes to your knees!

JOSEPH. I've tried it –

RICK. Yeah?

KEIRAN. So have I.

KEVIN. Haven't we all?

STEPHEN. Look at this! Even Kevin's done it! He's a priest! And you want to know why I'm so obsessed with size! It's like guys who don't have any money – it's all they fucking talk about.

RICK. I have a question. Who here has actually measured their dick?

*(They all raise their hands. Even **FATHER KEVIN**.)*

JOSEPH. I keep doing it – over and over – like it's going to get bigger when I'm not looking –

KEIRAN. I can't believe you've said that –

JOSEPH. You too?

*(**KEIRAN** nods. So does **STEPHEN**.)*

STEPHEN. Once a day for me –

RICK. Every Sunday night.

STEPHEN. Okay. So who used to think that if you jerked off a lot it would get bigger?

KEIRAN. A book I read *said* it would – !

JOSEPH. I think I read that book –

RICK. We *all* read that book –

STEPHEN. The other thing I've been wondering – do you think there's a support group for guys who are really hung?

RICK. What do *you* think?

KEIRAN. Makes you wonder what they would complain about –

KEVIN. Now come on – those guys have problems, too.

STEPHEN. Yeah, like buying extra-large condoms –

KEVIN. It's pretty well-documented most guys who are well-endowed can't get completely hard –

RICK. Boo hoo for them –

JOSEPH. When I see a guy walking down the street in a pair of tight jeans and he looks like he's got the Chrysler Building stuffed down there – I get a little queasy.

RICK. Maybe you're jealous –

STEPHEN. "Duh" –

JOSEPH. No, it's gross. You're scaring the children!

KEVIN. Okay, okay! You were finishing your story.

JOSEPH. The sex slowly stopped. I guess it does for a lot of folks after you've been married a while but – this was different – the affection stopped, too. I wanted sex. I wanted it everyday. But I was too afraid.

KEIRAN. You try therapy?

JOSEPH. It was too humiliating. "You see, Doctor, I have the world's smallest wiener and I can't satisfy my wife."

KEIRAN. Did you talk to your wife about it?

JOSEPH. Oh, we talked about it all the time. We talked it into the ground. But in the end, I didn't do anything about it.

KEIRAN. How'd you have the kids?

JOSEPH. We didn't stop completely. Every once in a while we would do it. We wanted a family.

(quietly)

She must have wanted something else all along.

STEPHEN. Well, she got it.

JOSEPH. All I know is what I hate most is being alone. Trying to raise my daughters by myself. Trying to explain why mommy left and why mommy doesn't want to see them again.

KEIRAN. That's bloody revolting –

JOSEPH. She wanted a new life. Those girls were a reminder of what she was desperate to forget –

KEIRAN. But to just walk away, to leave your husband of nearly twenty years, two beautiful girls –

KEVIN. You both must have been unhappy for a long time.

JOSEPH. That's why I can't get angry at her. I try. God, I try. But it was like when my own mother left. She did it to survive!

KEVIN. That doesn't make it any easier for you –

JOSEPH. I shoulda gone to that therapist – !

KEVIN. Shoulda, woulda, coulda...

(They sit with that a few moments.)

Anything else, Joseph?

JOSEPH. I'm just tired of being invisible. Top of my head. My job, my life! Between my legs.

KEVIN. I hear you.

JOSEPH. You?

KEVIN. *(realizing he's said too much)* Joseph, finish up. Keiran, do you have any more questions?

STEPHEN. You been holding out on us, Father?

KEVIN. Let's move forward.

STEPHEN. You finally gonna share something?

KEVIN. I said quite enough today –

STEPHEN. You barely opened your mouth!

KEVIN. Between the ethnic stereotype chanting and the confession about the ruler, I may be defrocked.

KEIRAN. Come on, Father – you can do it – it's just us fellas –

KEVIN. That's not why we're here.

KEIRAN. But the other lads –

KEVIN. I'm not the other lads, Keiran. My job is to run the group. It's not about me tonight.

KEIRAN. But –

KEVIN. You're on, Keiran. "Action."

KEIRAN. There was such a look of pain on your face. When you answered Joseph.

RICK. He's right, Father – there was –

STEPHEN. I saw it, too –

KEIRAN. It's always you jolly fellas – with your smiles – and jokes – is that why you're an actor, Father? 'Cause you get to be someone else?

KEVIN. No.

KEIRAN. None of us, except Rick here, much likes who we are. He works very hard at it.

KEVIN. Keiran –

KEIRAN. Do you like who you are, Father? Are you not answering because you don't want to lie?

KEVIN. I think we should move on –

KEIRAN. So fellas – Father's never stood up and talked about himself?

JOSEPH. It's usually just church stuff –

RICK. Acting auditions –

KEIRAN. Never anything personal?

STEPHEN. Are you kidding? I almost fell out of my chair when he made that crack about the ruler.

*(Silence. **KEIRAN** looks at **KEVIN**.)*

KEIRAN. You must want to say something. After all this silence. Go on, Father. Then I'll tell you about myself.

*(**KEVIN** takes a deep breath, sighs it out, then stands. It takes him a moment. There is a mixture of fear, relief and exhilaration on his face.)*

KEVIN. My name is Kevin Shaunessy, I'm fifty years old and I have The Irish Curse –

EVERYONE BUT KEVIN. Hello, Kevin!

KEVIN. *(relaxing into it; his humor returning)* My father was a Shaunessy. My mother was a Corrigan. The Curse did not pass over my house! I'm a Catholic priest in the Diocese of Brooklyn and a Franciscan father for almost thirty years –

KEIRAN. Very impressive –

KEVIN. *(enjoying himself now; taking the stage)* I was born in Boston, Mass, which is perhaps the only state in the Union where being stricken with the Irish Curse is not unusual. Massachusetts. Where the Pilgrims landed. The habitat of the Kennedys. And home to countless poor Irishmen who've suffered the same wretched fate as their ignominious forefathers – to be born prick-less!

RICK. Oh Father, come on –

KEVIN. The Irish are famous all over Southie for their non-existent dingers – it's part of their legacy –

STEPHEN. A fine actor and a drama queen as well –

JOSEPH. Father, you aren't seriously saying you don't have a *pecker* –

KEVIN. Only a *slight* exaggeration –

RICK. It could be true, he's never described it –

STEPHEN. Okay, okay. How small is it?

KEIRAN. Stephen, I can't believe you're asking a *priest* to tell you the size of his willie.

STEPHEN. Look, Irish Boy, you're the one making him do this. Don't change the rules 'cause he's a priest!

KEIRAN. Father, you don't have to get too specific –

KEVIN. These three men have bared their souls tonight – why shouldn't I?

KEIRAN. Christian modesty?

KEVIN. Fuck Christian modesty!

JOSEPH. I've never heard a priest say "fuck" –

KEVIN. You just did. The ground didn't open up. The church is still standing – so am I! What do you want to know, gentlemen?!

STEPHEN. Everything!

RICK. Shut up, Stephen! Whatever you want to tell us, Father –

STEPHEN. Don't leave *anything* out!

KEVIN. Where do you want me to start?

STEPHEN. I will repeat the question – "How small is it?"

KEVIN. As my father, may be rest in peace, used to say –
"'Tis the size of a bee's dick."

(The guys all break up.)

JOSEPH. Honestly, Father. "A bee's dick?"

KEVIN. As I said, a slight exaggeration. I must admit, for
the sake of full disclosure, there's not much, but what's
there is thick. I do have *girth*!

STEPHEN. Girth is good!!!

JOSEPH. I'd give my left nut for girth –

RICK. *(teasing)* I don't know, Father. You're a guy with girth.
We might have to ask you to leave –

STEPHEN. How wide is it? Can you get your fist around it?

KEVIN. Stephen –

RICK. This is like blowing my mind –

JOSEPH. I'll never be able to listen to you preach again –

STEPHEN. I'm still trying to see it in my head –

KEVIN. It's just another variation of the Curse –

KEIRAN. Father, you're a brave man –

KEVIN. Keiran, I want to thank you.

KEIRAN. Whatever for?

KEVIN. I suddenly find this all very liberating!

KEIRAN. Do you?

KEVIN. After all these years. Talking about it is fantastic –
saying the words out loud!

*(KEVIN looks at the guys and smiles. He launches in
with great enthusiasm.)*

I have had this stumpy little penis since I was twelve. I
used to dread gym class because of the showers. As I
said, South Boston is rife with The Curse but my penis
was so weird-looking even guys who were smaller made
fun of me!

KEIRAN. To distract from their own –

KEVIN. Because of all the teasing, I thought no woman
would ever want a poor fellow like me. So I made the
choice to change my life. I took what I thought was the
only road left. This!

(He points to his collar.)

JOSEPH. That's why there are so many Irish priests!

RICK. "Duh."

STEPHEN. You're one of the seven Catholic priests in the world who isn't gay?

KEVIN. Sorry, Stephen –

STEPHEN. Nothing? Never. Not even in the seminary?

KEVIN. Even if I had been, none of the fellas would have wanted me –

(teasing him)

I'm *Irish*!

STEPHEN. Even *seminarians*?!

KEVIN. The other guys in my class were Italian and Polish. Who do *you* think the gay guys went after?

RICK. It's an unfair world, Father –

STEPHEN. Okay, so you're straight. Did you ever have sex with a woman – before you went into the seminary?

JOSEPH. Stephen, for God's sake –

KEVIN. It's all right – it's good to be the star for once!

RICK. How old were you when you went in?

KEIRAN. Did you have a girlfriend?

STEPHEN. Did. You. Have. Sex?

KEVIN. There was one girl. She was Portuguese. Her family owned a bakery. She was beautiful. And Catholic. She was in love with me.

(takes a moment, acting it all out, loving the spotlight)

So there I was – at seventeen – after having suffered through all the teasing and laughing in the locker room – and there was this girl – and we liked each other – I thought, well, maybe it's okay after all – maybe girls don't care about stuff like that –

KEIRAN. That's what the magazines say. They interview women about what they like. The size of your willie's usually about number ten down the list –

JOSEPH. That's a big old lie – !

RICK. I don't think so. Angela and her friends said – women don't care about the size of a guy's dick – they respond to his *eyes* –

KEIRAN. His hair –

JOSEPH. Great…

RICK. His smile – his sense of humor –

KEIRAN. Whether he *listens* or not –

KEVIN. All I know is Lucy kept pressuring me to "do it." "I wanna do it," she'd say. "Let's do it." "All my *friends* are doing it." So we hid out in the storage room at the bakery. After it closed. We started fooling around on the floor and pretty soon we were covered all in white flour. I was kissing her and we were both going a little nuts and we got undressed and she had this gorgeous thin body and I was standing there with my stiffy. Well, she took one look at the "plump stump" and started shrieking. "Where's the rest of it?!! That can't be all!!! There's gotta be more!!!!"

(over the guys' loud reaction)

She didn't know any better. She came from a big family – she'd seen her brothers naked, I guess – apparently, they were all regular guys. I wish she had laughed. I would have been able to handle that. Because of the guys at school. She just shrieked. Like she was disgusted. Like it made her sick.

STEPHEN. That's always the worst –

(Everyone looks at him. He shrugs.)

One jerk who saw my cock said he'd come back when I grew up –

JOSEPH. One woman I slept with – before I got married –

KEIRAN. What, Joseph?

JOSEPH. It's the ultimate insult –

KEIRAN. What'd she say?

JOSEPH. That it was *cute*.

KEVIN. *(over the others' groans; taking stage again)* Anyway, Lucy finally quieted down and said she'd changed her mind and didn't want us to "do it." We stayed friends but the talk about us getting married stopped. Sometimes her friends would look at me funny – I didn't care – because by that time I'd gone to the parish priest and said I'd had a calling and that I wanted to go into the seminary. When he asked me if I was doing this because I really loved God – did I have any other reasons – was I running away or hiding out. I said no. I said I loved God with all my heart and soul and wanted to serve him and his people and the Holy Roman Catholic Church. Three weeks later, after graduation, I went to the seminary. I never looked back. Never kissed another girl. Never got laughed at again in a locker room. And now I've been a priest for twenty-odd years and the parishioners love me because I'm a great guy and I always know the latest jokes and the Church loves me because I don't molest little boys and don't have affairs with women and I am totally and completely dedicated to God.

KEIRAN. Ever have moments – of doubt?

KEVIN. In the beginning –

KEIRAN. What happened?

KEVIN. They went away. My family was so proud of me. I was making new friends. Men in the order, guys from the seminary. None of *them* ever laughed at me. None of *them* ever called me names.

KEIRAN. But are you angry at God – were you ever angry – that he let you down – ?

KEVIN. Look what he gave me instead, Keiran. This amazing life in this amazing city. Greatest city on earth –

STEPHEN. But you *are* angry, Kevin –

KEVIN. Yeah. I'm a man. I'm not perfect. Sometimes I think, why did I get shortchanged? Why me? The Irish Curse screwed up everything. I could have had a great wife, kids. A family. A home of my own. I have all *this* instead.

KEIRAN. Is it a fair trade?

(**KEVIN** *doesn't answer.*)

STEPHEN. I don't know about you, Kevin, but some days I'd sell my soul for seven fucking inches –

JOSEPH. I've had it all, Father. Everything you wanted. Now I've just got what's left. A cruddy apartment way, way uptown. A dead-end job. Piles of school bills, babysitter bills, clothing bills. And my girls. I wouldn't give them up for anything, but – *look what you've got!*

KEVIN. I thank God every day for it. And I curse him. For not giving me what I wanted. Not just seven inches, but that other whole life. Whatever it was.

(*silence*)

RICK. What did you say before, Keiran? "Fate's a funny thing."

KEIRAN. Aye.

KEVIN. Who knows, really, in the end? If I had a big prick, I might have *been* a big prick –

STEPHEN. Clichés are clichés…

KEVIN. Anything else, Keiran?

KEIRAN. Have you ever seen Lucy since?

KEVIN. She came to my 25th anniversary of my ordination.

KEIRAN. She say anything?

KEVIN. Just sat there in the back. She's fifty now. She runs the bakery back in Southie. Still trim, looks great. She has grandchildren.

RICK. And you got us.

(*Silence. They all sit there, thinking about their lives. Finally,* **RICK** *looks out the window.*)

RICK. Stopped raining.

STEPHEN. Finally –

JOSEPH. I got my car. If anybody needs a lift –

(*Sad silence. Quietly, with no fuss,* **KEIRAN** *stands.*)

KEIRAN. My name is Keiran Riley. I'm a roofer up in Queens. Working for my mother's business. She inherited from my Da. Who died last Easter. I've lived in America for four years. My brother, Sean, he came over first, he won a place, with the lottery. He sponsored us and brought us over. We're from just outside Dublin. I didn't know a thing about roofing until my father bought the business and we learned together.

(pause)

I met a girl, we were doing work on her family's townhouse, they live in Tribecca. She's a student. At NYU. She's studying banking and finance. We're engaged, actually. Have been for a year. She's the love of my life. The light of my life. The wedding's this Saturday. I'm still a virgin. My willie's so small I've been afraid to have sex with her. I'm afraid she'll call off the ceremony. I love her so much I could die.

(He starts to shake. **RICK** *stands as if to comfort him, but stops and looks at* **KEVIN**. *Before he can respond,* **KEIRAN** *starts to cry.* **JOSEPH** *immediately stands and puts his arms around* **KEIRAN**.*)*

STEPHEN. It's okay. It's okay.

JOSEPH. We've all been there, Keiran –

KEIRAN. What do I do? What do I do?

(The others stand there, as **JOSEPH** *holds* **KEIRAN**. *Finally, he stops crying.* **KEVIN** *helps* **KEIRAN** *back to his chair. The others mill around.)*

KEVIN. Steady yourself – come on –

KEIRAN. I don't know if I can –

KEVIN. Keiran, listen. We're only supposed to have the room for a few more minutes – we could go to my office and talk –

KEIRAN. I want to be here, Father, with the fellas –

KEVIN. Okay. But there's not much time left – try to pull yourself together –

KEIRAN. Okay. Okay.

(**STEPHEN** *kneels at* **KEIRAN**'*s side. Gently.*)

STEPHEN. Okay. So we're not gonna treat you any different from everyone else. You're gonna stand back up and tell us how big – or small – your little Irish cock is and you're gonna tell us how you feel about it and you're probably gonna cry some more – and then you're gonna let us help you –

RICK. The way you helped all of us –

KEIRAN. I didn't do anything for you –

RICK. Are you nuts? You kept asking all those questions –

KEIRAN. I just wanted to know what you'd all been through –

JOSEPH. We haven't talked about most of this stuff before – we just bitch a lot –

KEVIN. You were meant to come here tonight, Keiran –

STEPHEN. Oh stop the mystical woo-hoo-hoo –

RICK. I think Father's right –

STEPHEN. And I think you're full of shit!

JOSEPH. Stephen – would you do something for me?

STEPHEN. Yeah, what?

JOSEPH. Shut your nasty little self the fuck up!

STEPHEN. Up your ass, cracker –

KEVIN. Gentlemen –

JOSEPH. No, I mean it, this kid just stood here crying his eyes out and you were so kind and gentle with him and then you turned back into a little hell pig!

STEPHEN. A what?

JOSEPH. A hell pig!

RICK. I think it's a Southern for "asshole."

JOSEPH. No, no, we say *that*, too!

STEPHEN. All right, all right. I'm sorry, okay, Joseph! I live in New York. I'm cynical. Shoot me.

JOSEPH. Maybe that's something you ought try working on –

STEPHEN. Maybe you could stop whining so much and find a nice woman and take her out on a *date*!

JOSEPH. Maybe I will!

STEPHEN. Joseph, I swear – you go on a date – the next guy I blow, I'll ask his name!

JOSEPH. Deal.

(They shake hands. KEVIN stands.)

KEVIN. Let me tell the rummage sale ladies we need the room a little longer. I'll be right back –

(He exits. The guys are silent.)

KEIRAN. Rick?

RICK. Yeah?

KEIRAN. She really doesn't care? Angela?

RICK. Oh, Keiran – I don't know. She says she doesn't.

KEIRAN. The sex is good?

RICK. Yeah. I mean, I like it. She says she likes it. I gotta believe her.

KEIRAN. But Joseph said he had trouble – he slipped out –

JOSEPH. Not when we tried certain positions –

RICK. Like if she's on top –

KEIRAN. Right.

JOSEPH. One book I read – said if a guy is at least an inch – hard – he could have sex –

KEIRAN. Yeah?

JOSEPH. Yeah.

KEIRAN. Well –

RICK. I'm gonna say something really dumb –

KEIRAN. What's that?

RICK. If she loves you, it won't matter. Thinking like that has kept me going.

(Silence. KEVIN re-enters.)

KEVIN. The ladies are fine.

(KEVIN glances at KEIRAN. KEIRAN finally stands.)

KEIRAN. My name is Keiran Reilly and I have the Irish Curse –

THE OTHERS. Hello, Keiran –

KEIRAN. Hello, lads – it's funny, listening here tonight, how we define ourselves as men. I mean, if I saw any of you on the street, if I met you in a bar, I'd think, that fella is a man, all right – like Stephen here, he's tall and well-built and Jesus, he's a fine specimen. And this one, Rick, strong and sturdy and obviously a lad who loves his sport. This one, well, he's a successful lawyer and the proud father of two girls. And Kevin. A fine priest. Well-loved. Intelligent. And me – I've got a lovely fiancée who's smart as hell and adores me. I've helped support my family since I was seventeen. And I've got a good body – not from the gym, mind you, but from the hard work I do. I'm not a bad lad to look at. Back home I've had the ladies whistle at *me*! That's Dublin for you!

(taking a moment to continue)

Despite all that, I don't feel like a true man. Never have. I'm uncircumcised. Like most the lads back home. But even with the extra bit of foreskin, there isn't much there. No girth, like with Father Kevin. It is a tad larger than Joseph's bottle cap and a wee bit longer than Rick's baby corn. I've never actually seen a cocktail wiener so I can't say how I would measure up to Stephen. But all in all, even when it's hard, it's barely there. Maybe three inches –

JOSEPH. You got *us* all beat –

KEIRAN. Did I mention it's *thin*?

STEPHEN. How thin?

KEIRAN. 'Bout the width of an American nickel –

RICK. We had that in our family, too – my older brother – he got called "Stick Dick" –

KEIRAN. I've always hated my willie. *My* older brother used to refer to it as "Keiran's little williekin."

STEPHEN. Older brothers are shits –

KEIRAN. I tried to talk to my dad about it. It was just a fact of life, he said. Being small. His willie had served him well. Gave me and my brother life. Shouldn't grouse. Live with it! Then he'd drink himself into a bloody stupor.

KEVIN. I've always wondered – did drink cause The Curse – or do we drink because of it?

JOSEPH. I've wondered that myself –

KEIRAN. Do any of you have a problem with drink?

STEPHEN. A bit, yeah. Never at work.

JOSEPH. I gotta watch out for my girls –

RICK. Sometimes –

(They all look at **KEVIN**. *He just nods.)*

KEIRAN. One more Irish Curse. That's when I became obsessed with my size. It got worse when I came to America. I joined a gym and lasted a day. That locker room was a nightmare – all those fellas – with willies like stallions – that day, at the gym, I began to think the propaganda was true –

(grinning)

In America, everything is bigger!

STEPHEN. I hate those guys. Who walk around the gym naked. Ever notice it's always the guys with big dicks! Those guys who just can't seem to keep their towels on? The guys who linger in the hallway outside the shower, oh, for like twenty minutes, chatting away about their wives and their kids and their dogs – bare-assed – with this big old sausage swinging between their legs – *daring* you not to look – like we're gonna *miss* something like that!!!

(sheepishly; realizing he's gone off again)

Sorry.

KEVIN. When did you meet your girl, Keiran?

KEIRAN. 'Bout two years ago. She'd come up to the rooftop and watch us work. She'd sit there with a sun hat on, studying. I'd catch her smiling at me. After a week or so, she asked me to dinner –

JOSEPH. I love a woman who knows what she wants!

RICK. When did you know you were in love with her?

KEIRAN. We went to Tavern on the Green. She made me dance with her. Outside. Under the twinkling lights. . Slow dance. She fit in my arms. Custom made. I knew that night.

STEPHEN. That soon?

KEIRAN. Yeah. I guess. Yeah. There was this feeling in my chest. Like something had escaped. Something that had been locked up.

RICK. You were freed –

KEIRAN. Yeah.

(grinning)

You too?

RICK. Yeah. Oh yeah.

(They share a satisfied look.)

STEPHEN. But you never fucked her, right?

JOSEPH. You heard him. He's a virgin!

KEIRAN. Technically –

STEPHEN. You either are or you aren't –

KEIRAN. After Kelly and I went out a few times, we talked about having sex. She's a nice Catholic girl but like most Catholic girls – I had to put her off! Said I wanted to be a gentleman. She thought I was gay. I assured her I wasn't. Said I respected her and that I would like to wait until we were married. She wasn't keen on that but she agreed. Every now and then, she'd hint around she wouldn't mind if we did. She was honest. Told me she wasn't a virgin. I told her I was. That seemed to excite her.

KEVIN. Did you tell her *why* you were a virgin?

KEIRAN. I couldn't. Especially since she'd had experience. We did other things. Sexual things. Just never with my willie. When we finally decided to get married, I was in a frenzy. Being married meant sex. Real sex. I had to get some help. I went to bookstores, magazines racks, anything I could get my hands on. I'd sit at the computer for hours. Any website that had the word penis in it, I was there. I went to this one place – well, it's supposed to be for guys in our situation – to make you feel better – feel *normal* – I mean, the homepage has these pictures of guys with little willies – *little*? – Holy Mother of God, they're non-existent! I mean, I thought this page was supposed to make me feel better! I felt worse! Like I'm looking at this page of FREAKS!

(standing; nervous)

The worst part was, at the bottom of the page, there were these photos of fellas with huge willies – gigantic willies – titanic, *leviathan* willies – I didn't know willies came that big!

RICK. I've seen the website – it's an ad for doctors who do penis enlargements –

KEIRAN. Well, I'll tell you – it didn't sell me – there was this one fella – he had a fourteen inch willie – fourteen inches – *soft* – Jesus – !

STEPHEN. Not even I would want fourteen inches. Okay maybe for like five minutes –

KEIRAN. I ask you! Is that the sum total of what this poor lad's gonna be known for his *entire* life?

*(Silence. **KEVIN** looks his watch.)*

KEVIN. Better finish up.

KEIRAN. Well, as I said, since the engagement I've been looking for help. For almost a year. The wedding is Saturday. My willie's as tiny as it ever was. That's about all I have to say.

KEVIN. You sure?

(sensing something)

What?

KEIRAN. Nothing –

STEPHEN. Bullshit – there's something else – I'm a cop!

KEIRAN. Busted…

STEPHEN. *What else?*

KEIRAN. Well…

KEVIN. Go ahead, Keiran.

KEIRAN. I feel like everything in my life has built to this. To loving Kelly. Getting married. It's all I ever dreamed of. Being in America. Being a husband. A father. Being happy. The part I never thought about – the part I never considered – was that something like having a tiny willie – could ruin it all – That's why I'm so afraid. I'm *terrified*, lads! You can't know what's gone through my head this past week! Terrible things. Every time I look at her – or kiss her – or hear her voice – it's like I have this great bloody black demon inside me – saying I'm not good enough – saying "what makes you think she won't just walk away? Reject you? Laugh at you?!" What if she does reject me? What if she laughs? Or shrieks – like Kevin's girl did – or years from now, leaves me for some fella with a killer dick and a bloody vowel at the end of his name?

KEVIN. Keiran, you can't control what she's going to do –

KEIRAN. I know –

KEVIN. You gotta let it go –

KEIRAN. I can't – !

KEVIN. Why not?

KEIRAN. Because it would kill me if I lost her! I want to let her know what's going on inside. Why I feel the way I do. She sees it all in my eyes. The fear – I'm angry all the time – I'm jealous of every man we meet – I spend my days wanting to –

STEPHEN. Keiran – come on – take a breath –

KEIRAN. I can't! I'm paralyzed! I'm choking!

(**KEIRAN** *falls to his knees, overwhelmed. The guys surround him, helping him breathe.*)

KEVIN. From what you said, it doesn't sound like Kelly will reject you. It sounds like she loves you –

JOSEPH. Like she's nuts about you!

KEIRAN. But what if she *does* reject me?!

RICK. Keiran, would you really want to be with someone who'd reject you because of the size of your dick? I mean, come on, pal, how *little* do you think of yourself? That one thing – that one –

KEIRAN. "Tiny."

RICK. *Tiny* little thing is going to change her mind? How superficial do you think she is?

KEIRAN. But – and don't hate me for saying this, fellas – but I've sat here tonight and listened to you all talk about how your bloody lives have been ruined –

(*motioning to* **KEVIN**)

This one hid out in the priesthood –

(*pointing at* **STEPHEN**)

This doesn't know how to be intimate –

(*pointing at* **JOSEPH**)

This one is bitter and negative. And you –

RICK. What am I, Irish Boy?

KEIRAN. You lie about what a stud you are. You shove socks down your shorts and tell your mates you fuck every woman you meet. You act like you're brave and like you don't care but underneath – !!!!

RICK. But I haven't given up, have I? HAVE I???!!! These guys haven't either! Not a single goddamn one of them! They come here *every* week. They make the *effort*. They're *trying* to change. We're not all doing as well as we'd like but we're *here*!

JOSEPH. My daddy used to say that ninety percent of life is just showing up –

RICK. That's right, Joseph. That's right!

(*to* **KEIRAN**)

And having this night to look forward to – knowing there's a place we can go to and be together – and knowing that we are not alone – that gives us all a little hope. And a little hope can either do a lot of damage – or it can *save your goddamn life* –

KEIRAN. BUT I'LL STILL HAVE THE CURSE!!

RICK. The Irish Curse isn't having a wee willie, Keiran. It's letting that willie *define* your life – who you are and what you'll be – that's The Curse – so take your tiny little Irish baby dick and go home to your girl and just *love* her, for Christ's sake!!! Just love her!!! There's nothing else you can do! She's gonna make the decision, pal! It's outta your hands. All right?!

(**KEIRAN** *stares at* **RICK** *then looks at the others. They haven't liked hearing this but they aren't angry. A change comes over* **RICK**. *He relaxes.*)

And when you're in public wear a jock stuffed with a nice white cotton sports sock –

KEIRAN. Loosely rolled –

RICK. Tell Kelly you want help picking it out. Angela loves that. It's like the two of us pulling a fast one on the world.

(**JOSEPH** *leans in to* **KEIRAN**.)

JOSEPH. You gotta do this tonight. While you're still fired up. Talk to her. Tell her you're afraid. Tell her why. Be very, very clear –

KEIRAN. Oh Joseph –

JOSEPH. And tell her you'll do anything to make her happy. Tell her you'll go to a counselor – a therapist – buy her a G.D. dildo if that'll help!

STEPHEN. But draw the line at male escorts and three-ways.

KEIRAN. Is that all your advice, Stephen?

(**STEPHEN** *takes a moment to answer.*)

STEPHEN. Just don't lock yourself into one place. One way of thinking. That's the kiss of death. Things change. Let 'em.

(**KEIRAN** *looks at* **KEVIN**.)

KEVIN. Just make the rest of Kelly's life so wonderful she won't think of anything but how much she loves you.

(long silence)

KEIRAN. I've got to go. Kelly's probably frantic. She worries about me –

RICK. Lucky you –

KEIRAN. Nice feeling. Knowing someone's worried about you –

JOSEPH. Best in the world.

KEVIN. Anything else – ?

STEPHEN. Actually, yeah.

KEVIN. What's that?

STEPHEN. Keiran never said how *he* found us. Come on, "woof." Turnabout's fair play –

JOSEPH. You grilled the group –

RICK. So the group grills you.

KEVIN. Keiran?

*(It takes **KEIRAN** a moment, then –)*

KEIRAN. I was doing a job today over in Park Slope. A new roof on an old townhouse. Kelly called on my mobile at lunch to say she was concerned about me – I was so distant and cross all the time – she wanted to know if I was okay – if I still loved her – I said, "Yeah, of course" and rang off. She rang me back. Crying. Wanting to know what she had done wrong. "Nothing," I said, "except being a silly cow for loving me." Then I rang off –

(almost unable to continue)

After work I started for the Brooklyn Bridge –

STEPHEN. From Park Slope?

KEIRAN. It's a lovely walk – I've done it before –

JOSEPH. It was pouring rain all day –

KEIRAN. I'm used to working in the rain –

KEVIN. Why were you walking to the bridge?

(silence)

KEIRAN. My father used to tell about this fella – from Greece – who'd moved to Dublin – he'd been there a while – things were all wrong in his life – he didn't have a job – nor money to get home – he thought things would never go his way – so he started walking – toward a place he knew. When he was almost there, he realized he was lost. He'd walked down the wrong street. As he turned to go back, he heard voices through a window. People were speaking his language. He walked inside. It was a meeting of some kind – the people asked if they could help him – he answered back in his native tongue – "No, just, if you would, allow me to sit a while and be with you." They did. They sang songs and told stories and at the close of the meeting –

(almost overcome)

They asked him to join their group. Which he most gratefully did. Then they asked why he had happened to be there – how fortunate he had been walking down that particular street – and the lad said – "I was on my way to the bridge. To do away with myself. I heard your voices – in my own language – so I stopped a while before I went on."

(looking at the others)

It's a fine thing, the Brooklyn Bridge. Very high. Very high.

(Silence. The guys are overwhelmed.)

STEPHEN. It was really that bad?

KEIRAN. In my mind –

JOSEPH. I've never felt that low before –

RICK. My bro did.

KEIRAN. I was turned around and couldn't find the bridge. The first person I asked for directions was Father Kevin. He told me he was on his way to this group –

KEVIN. I wasn't going to tell him what the group was for. Something inside just said – "Oh fuck it!"

*(**KEIRAN** shakes hands with **RICK** and **JOSEPH**.)*

KEIRAN. Rick. Joseph.

*(**KEIRAN** goes for his things. **STEPHEN** hands him his backpack and coat.)*

STEPHEN. Here.

KEIRAN. Thank you, Stephen.

KEVIN. One last thing –

KEIRAN. Yes, Father?

KEVIN. Promise you'll be back next week –

KEIRAN. You fellas are a fine lot. But I won't be here –

(over their groans)

God willing – I'll be on my bloody *honeymoon!*

(Over their grins; he is one of them now.)

I'll be back the week after. *And* the week after that. And that, lads, is a solemn promise from a baby-dicked Irishman! Good night!

(With great dignity, he walks out of the room. The others stand there, allowing the enormity of what has happened wash over them. They slowly start to share looks among themselves. The silence is overwhelming. There is almost something holy about it. Then the lights start to fade.)

(Curtain)

PROPERTY, COSTUME AND SET LIST FOR "THE IRISH CURSE"

PROP LIST

iPhone (Stephen)
Broken umbrella (Stephen)
Newspaper (Stephen)
Back pack (Rick)
Smoothie or vitamin water (Rick)
Power bar (Rick)
Cell phone (Rick)
Briefcase (Joseph)
Umbrella (Joseph)
Wallet (Joseph)
Cell phone (Joseph)
Wallet (Joseph)
Back pack (Keiran)
Cell phone (Keiran)
Wallet (Keiran)
Pen (Kevin)
Carton of Milk – for coffee (Kevin)
Water Cooler (set dressing)
Coffee maker (set dressing)
Cups (set dressing)
Sugar (set dressing)
Napkins (set dressing)
Stir sticks (set dressing)
Paper towels (set dressing)
Money collection can (set dressing)
Sign up sheet on a clipboard (set dressing)
Trash Can (Set dressing)

COSTUME LIST

STEPHEN – leather jacket, polo shirt, jeans, boots
RICK – sweat pants, Yankees t-shirt, zip up windbreaker, running shoes, sports baseball cap, yellow rain poncho
JOSEPH – inexpensive suit pants and coat, dress shirt, tie, inexpensive rain coat, Inexpensive dress shoes
KEVIN – plain black pants and shirt, black dress shoes, cardigan sweater, Roman collar
KEIRAN - button down work t-shirt, work pants, heavy work boots, hoodie, coat

SET PLOT

The play was written to be done simply, with seven or eight inexpensive folding chairs, a table for the coffee maker (or just a Sparkletts water dis-perser, as was done at the Edinburgh Festival), a hanging window frame and a door frame for entrances.

Or —

It can be done as it was off-Broadway, with a completely realistic Brooklyn church basement set. This included a working door with a crash bar up stage left which lead out to the street, and an arched, open exit up stage right, leading to a hallway and the rectory. There was a bank of stained glass windows along the back wall. There was also a rain box above the windows, which allowed dripping rain water to be visible to the audience. If you are aiming for super realism, it would be handy to have a bulletin board up on one wall, covered in church flyers. There can also be a roll-ing rack against the back wall to hold the coats which the actors take off when they enter. Last but not least, a table along the wall stage right can hold all of the makings for the coffee the guys drink, the clipboard with the group sign-up sheet and a small basket for donations to the group. The gorgeous original set, by Lauren Helpern, even had four set of steam pipes going up the molded stone walls, which every self-respecting, old Catholic Church basement in Brooklyn would absolutely have. Toss in a linoleum floor, some cardboard boxes marked "Rummage Sale" and a banner announcing the same Rummage Sale and you'll be ready to go.

Whatever you do, once the guys set up the five or six folding chairs at the top of the show, that should be the centerpiece of your playing area.

SOUND

For the first ten minutes or so of the show –especially when someone opens the door from the outside – we should hear the sound of rain. Don't overdo it, but we should really hear it. It should fade away during the play, so that near the end, when someone remarks that it has stopped, we should feel the absence of the rain. The rain can be mixed in with street sounds, car honks, etc. Finally, it's nice to hear church bells just before the meeting starts, and in the silence when the rain stops.

A FEW OTHER NOTES

The first three guys (Joseph, Rick and Steven) should be wet when they come into the meeting. Really, really wet. Keiran should also be very wet when he comes in. Fr. Kevin should be dry.

The guys should sound like they are from different places, but don't make the play about accents and dialects. Except Keiran. He must have a proper Dublin accent.

ELEPHANT SIGHS

Ed Simpson

Comedy / 5m

Not long after moving to the small town of Randolphsburg, PA, uptight lawyer Joel Bixby is invited by Leo Applegate, an avuncular fast food connoisseur, to join a group of townsmen who meet in a ramshackle room at the edge of town. Leo has chosen Joel as a replacement for the late - and greatly beloved – Walter Deagon. Despite protesting that he's just not an organizational man, Joel finds himself mesmerized by Leo's ebullient manner and agrees to drop by - without ever asking just what exactly it is the group actually does. Determining that the meeting will at least help him network with potential clients, Joel arrives, hoping that the group's purpose will eventually become clear. Joel's confusion only increases as, one by one, he meets the group's surviving members who includes Dink, a perpetually gleeful little man who deeply loves his bald-headed wife and who is "in touch with his feminine side"; insurance man Perry, a former minister in the midst of a painful crisis of faith; and Nick, a volatile contractor who has recently lost his job and family and is desperately looking for some kind of miracle. As an increasingly anxious Joel is swept up in the strange lives of the guys, he struggles to figure out exactly why they've all come together. The more time he spends with them, the more apparent it becomes that each of them are just as lost as Joel. As the evening progresses, however, the regulars - and newcomer Joel - grapple with their own disappointments, offer comfort to each other, and, in the process, finally reveal the mysterious reason for their gathering. A group of delightful characters highlight this comedy about loss, loneliness, and the healing power of friendship.

"Critic's Choice...Ed Simpson's riotous new male bonding comedy *Elephant Sighs* is deceptively unassuming....The mostly blue-collar characters speak in a hilarious hybrid of uneducated obtuseness and politically correct buzz words. Don't let the surface banality fool you. The emotions of these men, however imperfectly communicated, are agonizing, their need for comfort and companionship as acute as hunger and thirst."
- F. Kathleen Foley, *Los Angeles Times*

OTHER TITLES AVAILABLE FROM SAMUEL FRENCH

MEN OF TORTUGA

Jason Wells

Drama / 5m

Four men conspire to defeat a despised opponent by a ruthless act of violence: they will fire a missile into a crowded conference room on the day of an important meeting. Maxwell, a hero of the old guard, volunteers to sacrifice himself for the plan. Then Maxwell meets Fletcher, an idealist with a "Compromise Proposal" designed to resolve all conflicts. Maxwell regards the Compromise as hopeless, but he develops a liking for Fletcher - a distressing fact when Maxwell learns that, if the conspiracy proceeds, young Fletcher will be among the dead.

As the scheme spins wildly into complication, the plotters descend into suspicion, bloodlust and raucous infighting, while Fletcher is drawn, inexorably, into the lion's den.

"Jason Wells isn't giving everything away in his captivating new play *Men of Tortuga*. In addressing some serious contemporary issues, he creates a scenario where the audience has only a rough idea of what's going on. And that's just about the way it should be. In a crackling world premiere at the Asolo Repertory Theater, Wells tells a story of corporate greed, power, surveillance and the secrecy that increasingly pervades our daily lives. Wells and the Asolo cast grab the audience from the start...The play pulses with energy..."
-Variety

"...Gripping...You'll be hearing more about *Men of Tortuga*, a blistering new play about corporate and government malfeasance from a Chicago actor named Jason Wells (who turned in the best piece of writing all year from a playwright.)...On one level, Jason Wells' elliptical drama *Men of Tortuga* is a genre-based thriller a la James Bond or Quentin Tarantino. But Wells is sufficiently skilled to dig deeper than that....taut sophistication..."
- Chicago Tribune

www.ingramcontent.com/pod-product-compliance
Lightning Source LLC
Chambersburg PA
CBHW070649120726
47909CB00004B/1649